CW00867616

LANCASHIRE
EDUCATION COMMITTEE
BROADFIELD
SCHOOL

Thomas Nelson and Sons Ltd
Nelson House Mayfield Road
Walton-on-Thames Surrey
KT12 5PL UK

51 York Place
Edinburgh
EH1 3JD UK

Thomas Nelson (Hong Kong) Ltd
Toppan Building 10/F
22A Westlands Road
Quarry Bay Hong Kong

Thomas Nelson Australia
102 Dodds Street
South Melbourne
Victoria 3205
Australia

Nelson Canada
1120 Birchmount Road
Scarborough Ontario
M1K 5G4   Canada

© Templar Publishing Ltd 1985
First published by Hamlyn Publishing 1985
Second and subsequent impressions published by Thomas Nelson & Sons Ltd from 1989

Letterland was devised by Lyn Wendon and is part of
the *Pictogram* system © Lyn Wendon 1973-1986

ISBN 0-17-410153-8
NPN 20 19 18 17 16 15 14 13 12 11 10

Printed in Italy

All rights reserved. No paragraph of this publication may be reproduced, copied or transmitted
save with written permission or in accordance with the provisions of the Copyright, Design and
Patents Act 1988, or under the terms of any licence permitting limited copying issued by the
Copyright Licensing Agency, 90 Tottenham Court Road, London W1P 9HE.

Any person who does any unauthorised act in relation to this publication may be liable to criminal
prosecution and civil claims for damages.

Dippy Duck Dresses up

Written by
Jane Launchbury & Richard Carlisle

Illustrated by
Jane Launchbury

Nelson

One day Dippy Duck was having dinner when there was a knock on her Duck Door.

Dippy saw a big, red card appear through her letterbox. It landed on the doormat.

Dippy stopped eating and picked it up. "Dear Dippy," said the card, "please come to a Fancy Dress party tonight!"

Dippy Duck was delighted. She loved dressing up.

Dippy thought and thought about different ways of dressing up.

She thought of dressing up as a donkey, but decided she didn't have enough legs.

She thought of dressing up as a dragon, but decided her tail was too short.

"I will go and look in my dressing up drawer," she decided. "There's bound to be something good in there."

The first thing Dippy found was a pair of dark sun-glasses. She put them on.

Then she found an old hat and an old coat. She put them on too.
She also found a feather duster.
"This will do for a beard," she thought.

When she looked in the mirror, Dippy was delighted with her disguise. "I look just like a detective," she said to herself. "Now all I need is something to cover up my duck feet."

So she dived back into the drawer to find some boots to wear.

Soon it was time to leave for the party. Dippy was very excited as she set off down the path through the woods.

She thought of all the delicious food there would be to eat. That made her hungry.

Then she thought she heard a strange noise. She peered into the darkness of the wood, but there was nothing to be seen.

"Now's my chance to be a real detective," decided Dippy. So she crept through the bushes to take a closer look.

What she found made her rather frightened. Poking out from behind a big bush was a long spiky tail. It was covered in spots and when Dippy poked it, it wriggled from side to side.

"This looks dangerous," thought Dippy. She tried to remember if any of the other animals in Letterland had such a funny tail—but she couldn't think of a single one.

Dippy had to find out more about this strange beast. So she peeked round the bush.

There, standing right in front of her, was a huge animal. It had a long thin neck and a tiny head. All down it's back were big diamond-shaped spines.

There was no doubt about it … it was definitely a DINOSAUR!
Dippy Duck felt dizzy. The dinosaur looked so frightening.

Dippy wondered if dinosaurs ate ducks. "I do hope they don't!" she said to herself.

Dippy Duck was about to run
away, when she realised that
the dinosaur wasn't alone.

Standing nearby was a donkey with
funny legs that seemed to go in
different directions … and a doctor
with a rather large nose, dressed in
a smart white coat.

Dippy Duck began to see more and
more rather odd looking people and
animals.

There was even a dragon who was
trying to hide behind a tree.

Then Dippy Duck saw a big
table covered with lots and lots
of food. Everyone was helping
themselves … even the dinosaur!

At last Dippy realised where she was.
This was the Fancy Dress party!
It was being held in the woods!

Dippy Duck was most relieved. Now
instead of being frightened, she
began to wonder who everyone was
behind their disguise.

J ust then, the spiky-tailed dinosaur came up to her and said, "We've all decided that we need your help."

"Why me?" asked Dippy Duck. "Because you are a detective!" said the dinosaur. "That means you can help us find out who everyone is!" "Oh," laughed Dippy. "All right!"

Dippy Duck started to look at everyone more closely. She looked at the doctor's face, but she couldn't recognise him. Then she looked down at his feet … she was sure she had seen those feet somewhere before. Then she guessed!

You are the Hairy Hat Man!"
she cried. And he was. Then
she studied the donkey. What
were those golden strands of hair
poking out from the donkey's neck?
It didn't take Dippy long to work out
that the front end of the donkey was
Golden Girl and the back end was
Naughty Nick.

Soon she had guessed who nearly
everyone was, even the terrible
looking dragon. She was really the
Wicked Witch. There was only one
left—the dinosaur…Who could it be?

Dippy thought she knew, but just as
she was about to speak, the Hairy
Hat Man appeared with all the Fancy
Dress prizes.

Here we have a prize for the best disguise," said the Hairy Hat Man. "I think it should go to the dinosaur because nobody can guess who he is!"

"Wait a minute," yelled Dippy Duck, "I think it's really Eddy Elephant." And sure enough it was. "But he should still get the prize," she added. "Oh thank you," smiled Eddy. "And here's a special prize for you—for being such a good detective."

"How wonderful," said Dippy, and she really was delighted.
"Next time there's a Fancy Dress party," she thought to herself,
"I shall dress up as a detective again!"

THE END